# ROCK STAR SANTA

## BY GAYLE C. KRAUSE
## ILLUSTRATED BY WILL TERRY

SCHOLASTIC INC.
NEW YORK  TORONTO  LONDON  AUCKLAND  SYDNEY
MEXICO CITY  NEW DELHI  HONG KONG  BUENOS AIRES

For Marie Cimino, my biggest fan
—G.C.K.

For my family, for putting up
with all the long hours
—W.T.

ISBN-13: 978-0-545-08449-9
ISBN-10: 0-545-08449-0

Text copyright © 2008 by Gail Krause
Illustrations copyright © 2008 by Will Terry

12 11 10 9 8 7 6 5 4 3 2 1    8 9 10 11 12 13/0

Printed in the U.S.A.
First printing, December 2008

Rock the house. Rock the house.
Don't be quiet like a mouse.
Guitar licks and jammin' drums—
Rock the house when Santa comes!

Footlights shine. Tree is lit.
Play it like you'll never quit.

Sleigh bells ring above the noise.
Santa's bringing more than toys.
Children clap and yell and scream
When they first see Santa's team.
Stomping joins the loud applause.
Rock the house for Santa Claus!

Donner plays electric bass.
Blitzen wears a painted face.

Comet shoots across the stage.
Hip-hop Dancer's all the rage.

Dasher croons into the mikes.
Vixen wears her hair in spikes.

Cupid's jazzy kisses jingle.
Stage is set for old Kris Kringle.

Lights go up. Guitars blast.
It's Christmas now, not Christmas past!
Singing backup, Prancer's slick.
Spotlight centers on St. Nick.

Red silk scarf hangs from his neck.
In sequined vest he is bedecked.
Snow-white hair in ponytail,
Santa's ready. Watch him wail!

He marks the beat, looks at the crowd.
Now it's time, scream REALLY LOUD!
He grabs the mike, takes one step back
And . . . POOF!

The Christmas stage goes black!

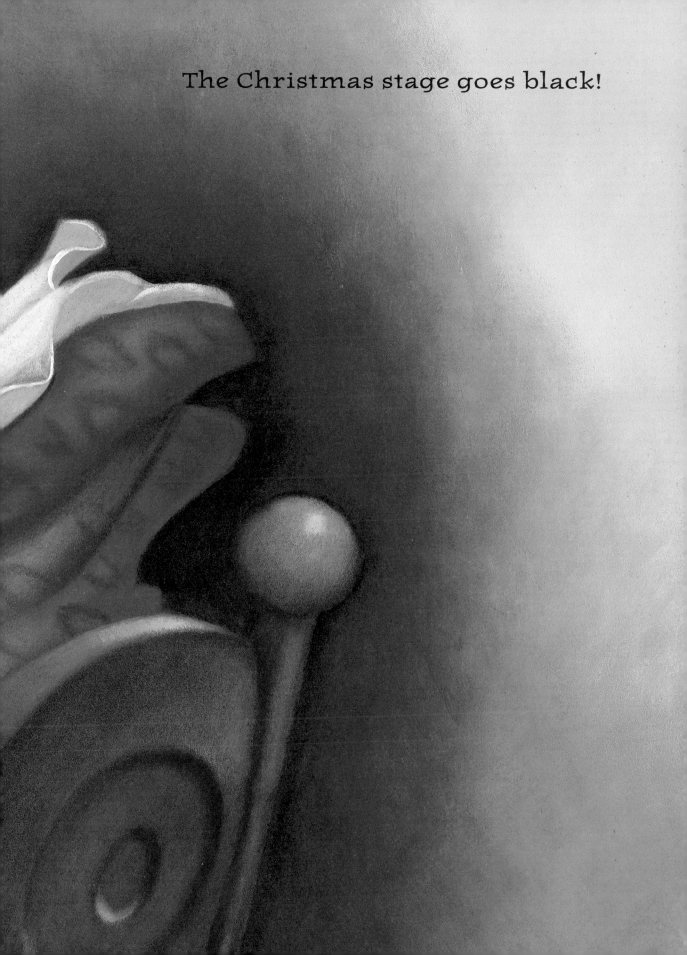

The Christmas concert felt so real.
I heard the children screech and squeal.
I saw Santa dancing there,
While silver snowflakes filled the air.

I must have dreamed this awesome sight,
'Cause Santa flies throughout the night,
Bringing all his special toys
On Christmas Eve to girls and boys.

But getting dressed on Christmas morn,
Inside my jeans, a ticket, torn.
Green spangles glimmer on the floor.
A long red scarf hangs from my drawer.

My window glints with frosted ice.
Peering through, I must look twice.
A silver snowflake flitters there,
Gleaming in the crisp, cold air.

Beside the flake, a written phrase
That keeps me in my Christmas daze.

On Christmas Eve,
I am the man.
Merry
Christmas
to my
biggest fan!
Love,
SANTA